Messy Bessey's
School Desk

By Patricia and
Fredrick McKissack

Illustrated by Dana Regan

Children's Press®
A Division of Grolier Publishing
New York · London · Hong Kong · Sydney · Danbury, Connecticut

To all the kids who made this title their first choice
—P. and F. M.

To Tommy and Joe
—D. R.

READING CONSULTANT
Linda Cornwell
Learning Resource Consultant
Indiana Department of Education

Library of Congress Cataloging-in-Publication Data
McKissack, Patricia.
    Messy Bessey's school desk / by Patricia and Fredrick McKissack ;
illustrated by Dana Regan.
        p. cm. — (A rookie reader)
    Summary: When Messy Bessey starts to clean up her desk at
school, she inspires the rest of the class to clean up the entire room.
    ISBN 0-516-20827-6 (lib. bdg.)   0-516-26361-7 (pbk.)
    [1. Orderliness—Fiction. 2. Schools—Fiction. 3. Stories in rhyme.]
I. McKissack, Fredrick. II. Regan, Dana, ill. III. Title. IV. Series.
PZ8.3.M224Me 1998
[E] —dc21   97-13837
                                    CIP
                                     AC

Printed in China.
20 21 22 23 24 R 21 20 19 18 17   62

Scholastic Inc., 557 Broadway, New York, NY 10012.

Messy, Messy Bessey,
your school desk is a mess.

There's wadded-up tissue
and paper clips,
colored markers
with dried-out tips,

VOTE FOR BESSEY

an old sack lunch,
a forgotten note,
scissors, tape, and
a poem you wrote.

Your desk is so messy, Bessey.
See broken crayons, pencils, too,
library books that are overdue,

rubber bands
and an apple core,
late homework
and so much more.

Messy Bessey had to agree.
Her desk was a disgrace.

So she threw away
the useless things, and
straightened out her space.

Bessey's desk was tidy now,
but something wasn't right.

AMY
FOR

There were other messy desks that were a terrible sight.

Come on, everybody.
Let's clean up your desks, too.

20

21

Bessey got the trash can
and showed them what to do.

23

Now all our desks are neat and clean.
Our papers and books are straight.

With everybody helping,
our classroom looks just great.

Cheers, Miss Bess!

Your leadership was excellent.

That is why we elected you
to be class president.

Word List (111 Words)

a	classroom	helping	now	showed	to
agree	clean	her	old	sight	too
all	clips	homework	on	so	trash
an	colored	is	other	something	up
and	come	just	our	space	useless
apple	core	late	out	straight	wadded
are	crayons	leadership	overdue	straightened	was
away	crayons	let's	paper	tape	wasn't
away	desk	library	papers	terrible	we
bands	desks	looks	pencils	that	were
be	disgrace	lunch	poem	the	what
Bess	do	markers	president	them	why
Bessey	dried	mess	right	there	with
Bessey's	elected	messy	rubber	there's	wrote
books	everybody	Miss	sack	things	you
broken	excellent	more	school	threw	your
but	forgotten	much	scissors	tidy	
can	got	neat	see	tips	
cheers	great	note	she	tissue	
class	had				

About the Author

Patricia and Fredrick McKissack are freelance writers, editors, and owners of All-Writing Services, a family business located in Chesterfield, Missouri. They are award-winning authors whose titles have been honored with the Coretta Scott King Award, the Jane Addams Peace Award, and the Newbery Honor. Pat's book *Miranda and Brother Wind*, illustrated by Jerry Pinkney, was a 1989 Caldecott Honor Book.

The McKissacks have written other Rookie Readers® about Messy Bessey—*Messy Bessey, Messy Bessey and the Birthday Overnight, Messy Bessey's Closet, Messy Bessey's Garden,* and *Messy Bessey's Holidays.* They have three grown children and live in St. Louis County, Missouri.

About the Illustrator

Dana Regan was born and raised in northern Wisconsin. She migrated south to Washington University in St. Louis, and eventually to Kansas City, Missouri, where she now lives with her husband, Dan, and her sons, Joe and Tommy.